MY FIRST

Sticker Art

make
believe
ideas

Welcome to My First Sticker Art!

Have fun finishing the pictures using your shape stickers.

1 Find the sticker sheets at the back of the book.
There are circles, squares, rectangles, and triangles.

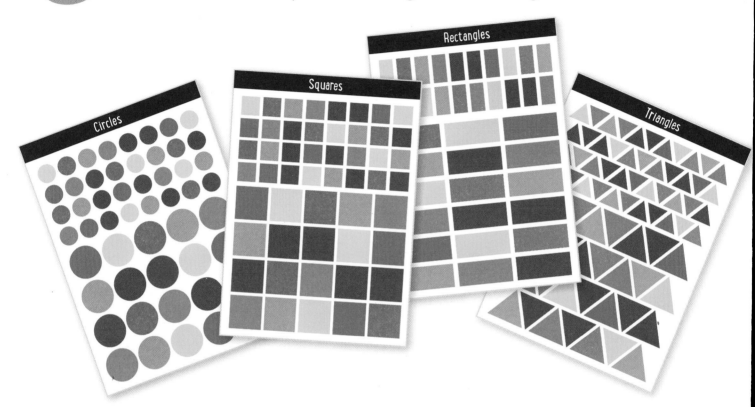

2 Look at the pictures. The key at the top tells
you which shapes you will need for that page.

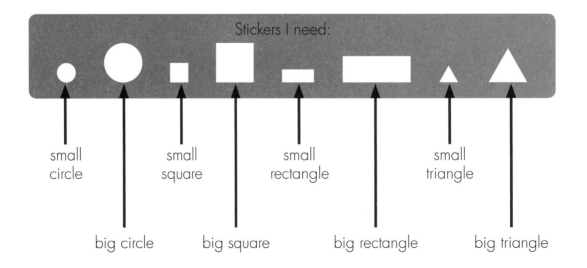

Stickers I need:

small circle

big circle

small square

big square

small rectangle

big rectangle

small triangle

big triangle

3 Find the shape and choose the right size. Pick any color you want! When you are sure you have found the right sticker, carefully peel it off and stick it down.

Check the shape when you have placed each sticker.

small circle

big circle

4 The pictures begin by focusing on one shape. At the end of the book, you will need different shapes to finish the pictures.

Have fun!

Playful puppy

Stickers I need:

Woof!

Woof!

Fluttery butterflies

Home, sweet home

Time to play!

Stickers I need:

Colorful crayons

Point to your favorite color!

Making music

Ding!

Ding!

Ding!

Whirring helicopter

Stickers I need: ▲ ▲

Cute kitten

Stickers I need:

Fruit friends

The creepy-crawlies are having a picnic!

Stickers I need:

Clean and dry

Stickers I need:

All aboard!

Stickers I need:

Have you been on a train?

Stickers I need:

Choo!

Choo!

Stickers I need:

Tweet!

Under the sea

Stickers I need:

Point to the jiggly jellyfish!

Stickers I need:

Rocking robots

Stickers I need:

Bop!

Whizz!

Stickers I need:

Clunk!

Let's dance!

Flower garden

Stickers I need:

Stickers I need:

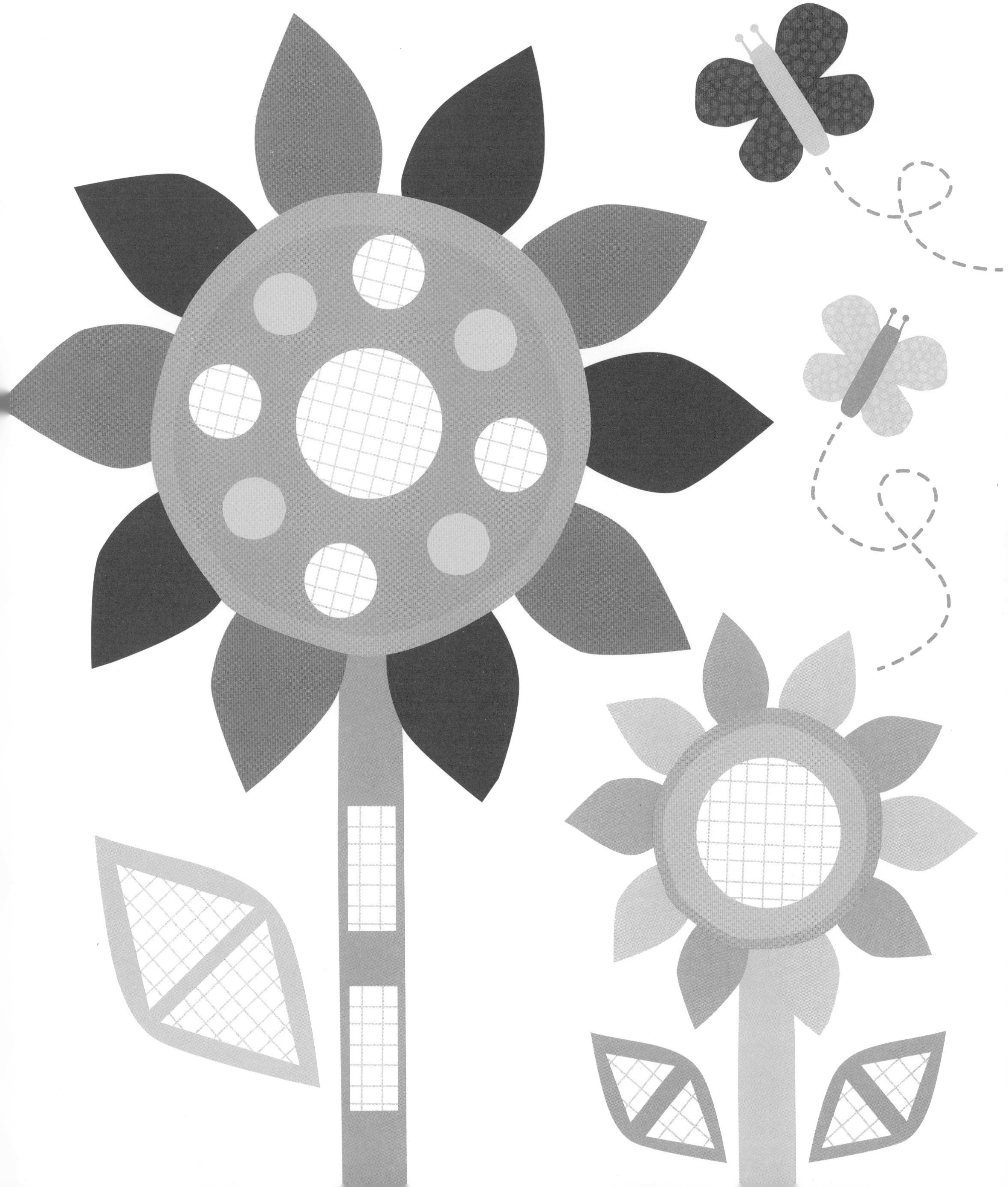

Super space

Stickers I need:

Can you see the moon?

Sweet treats

Stickers I need:

milk
Choco

Stickers I need:

Whoosh!

Animal party

In the city

Stickers I need:

On the move

Vroom!

Stickers I need:

Beep!

Funny dinos

Point to the dinosaur's egg!

Stickers I need:

See you soon!

Stickers I need:

Circles

Rectangles

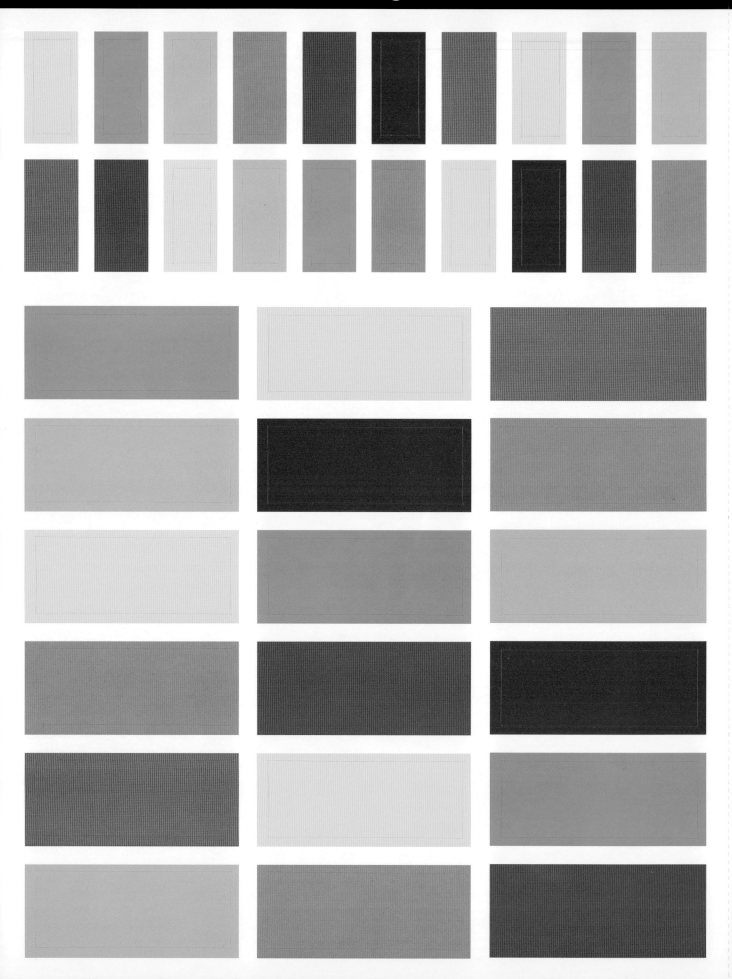

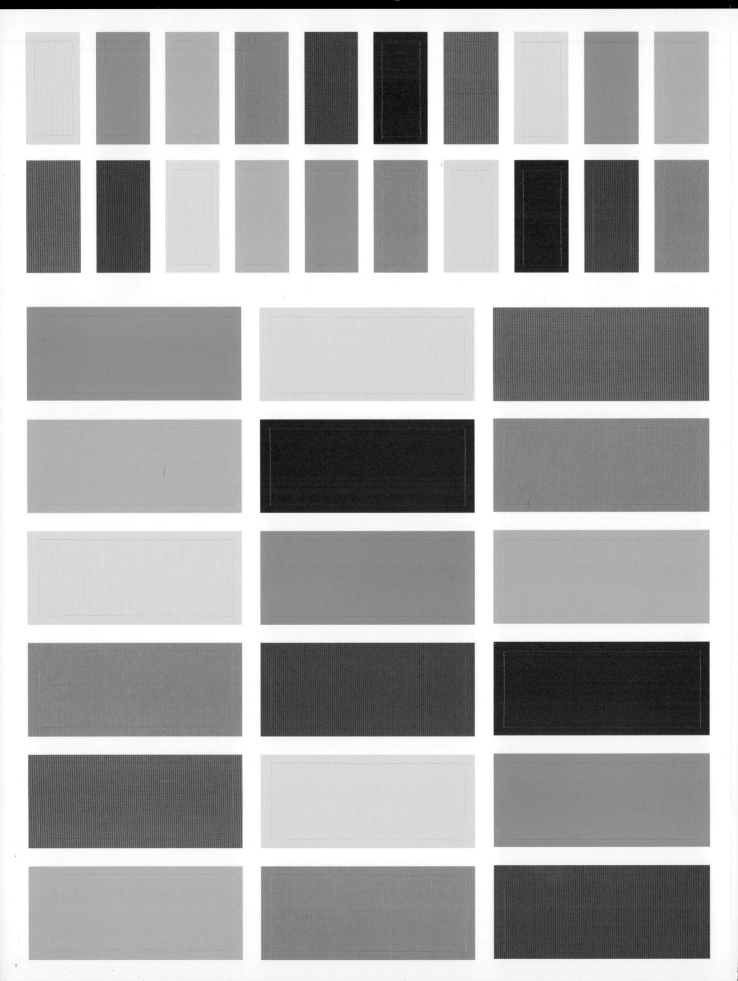

Triangles

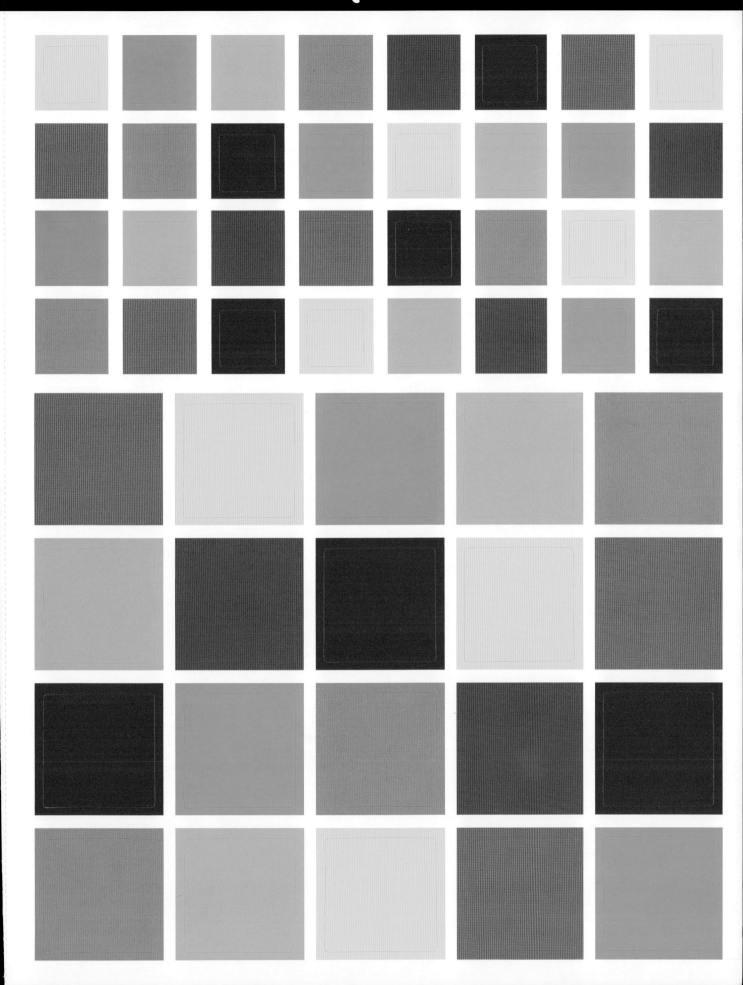

Squares